The Adventures of Jack and Machu:
Jack the Kitten is Very Brave

by Tabitha Grace Smith

Illustrated by Mindy Lou Hagan

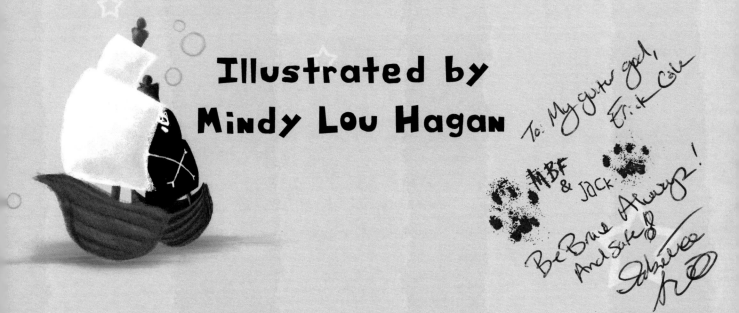

Special thanks to Kim, Emma,
Clay, Cliss, Brian
& the Flock of Awesome Coolness.

For the real life Machu (aka Myboyfriend) & Jack,
inspiring me since 2005.
For mom and dad, thanks for being such awesome parents.
And for Isabella & Heidi, Greyson, and Elanor, never
forget how much you're loved.
- TGS

For my family, because I wouldn't have gotten this far
without you.
And to Janice, because I've never forgotten.
- M.L.H.

Jack is a pirate and he loves everything about being a pirate.

Everything that is, but water.

Jack loves playing with swords. He loves searching for buried treasure. And he is fond of saying, "Argggggh!"

But Jack is very scared of water.

Machu, his older brother, was NOT afraid of the water!

In fact Machu was IN the bathtub!

Jack just sat ON the edge.

"Come play with me!" Machu said.
"There's lots of great toys in here."

Jack flicked his tail.
"You could give me some of them."

"No," Machu said.

"These are just bath toys.
You can't play with them out there.
You need to come in here."

Jack watched Machu play and splash in the water.

Jack decided to pretend the edge of the bathtub was a pirate's plank.

Jack walked UPPPP the plank.

Jack walked
DOWN the plank.

He said. "Arggggh!
Walk the plank matey!"

Jack pretended
very well.

but it didn't look as fun as
Machu's boats.

"Come play with me!" Machu said again. "You can be the pirate boat. And I will be the good guys. And I will chase you."

Jack was still scared of the water.

He decided to try putting just ONE paw into the water.

He reacccccchhhhhhhhhhhhed down slowly and dipped in his paw.

There was a
SPLASH!

It was a funny feeling, so Jack
laughed. The bubbles in the bathtub
moved. Jack pawed the bubbles
again and giggled.

Machu laughed at his little brother.
Then he made a bubble hat.

"Oh!!!" Jack said.
"May I have one?"
"Of course!" Machu said.
"That's good asking!" Machu made
Jack a bubble hat. Jack bent down
so Machu could reach.

Machu brought the pirate boat closer to the edge.

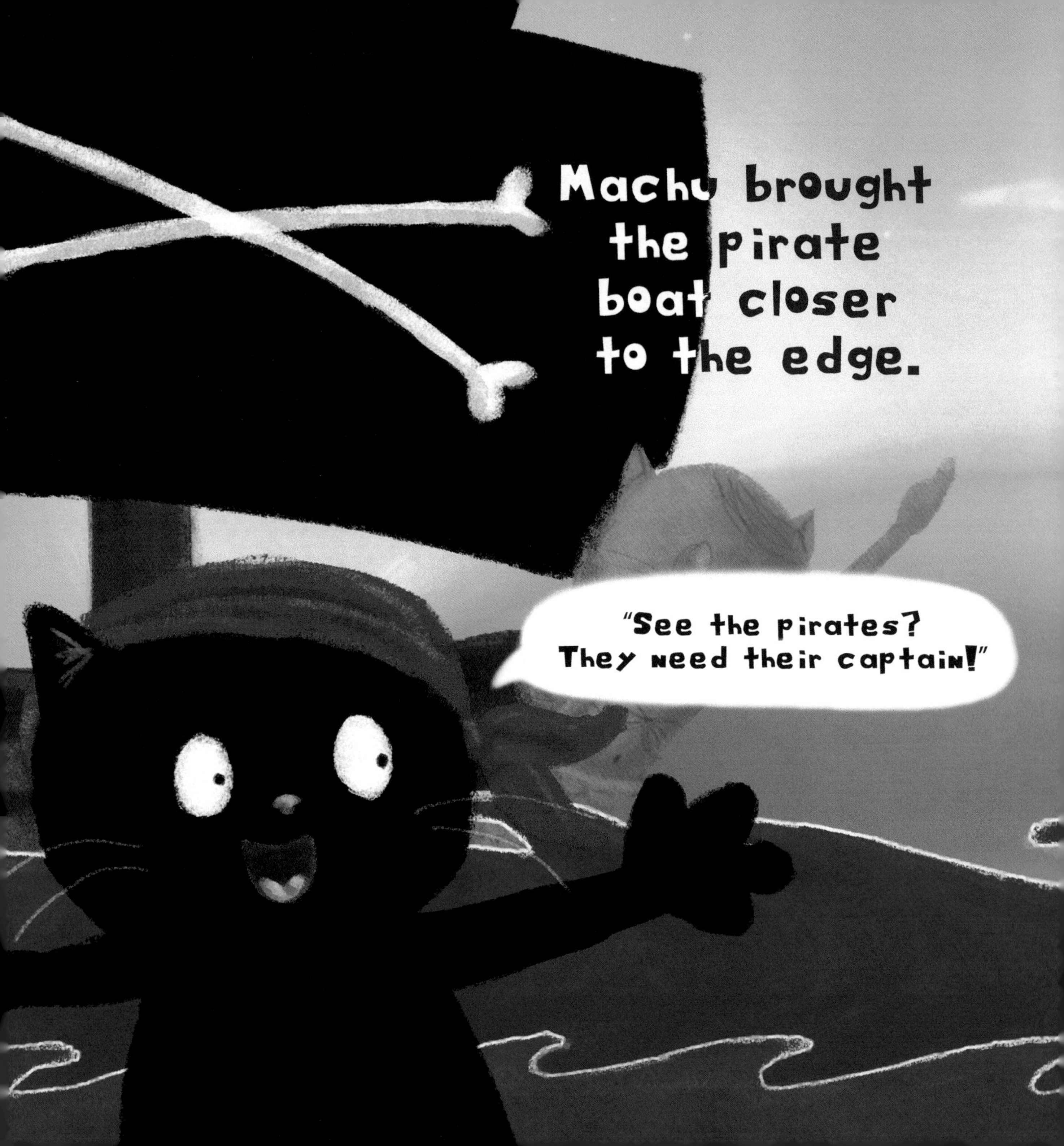

"*Avast!*" Jack said.

It was a very piratey thing to say.

Jack pushed on the boat and listened to the ripples of the water.

"ARRRGHHH!" Jack said with his best pirate growl. "Ahoy me harties!"

Jack pushed the boat forward and back. Machu's boat steamed ahead and chased the pirate ship. "We'll get you Captain Jack!"

Jack the Pirate Captain was NOT afraid. "Fire canons!" Jack said! and he splashed at Machu's boat.

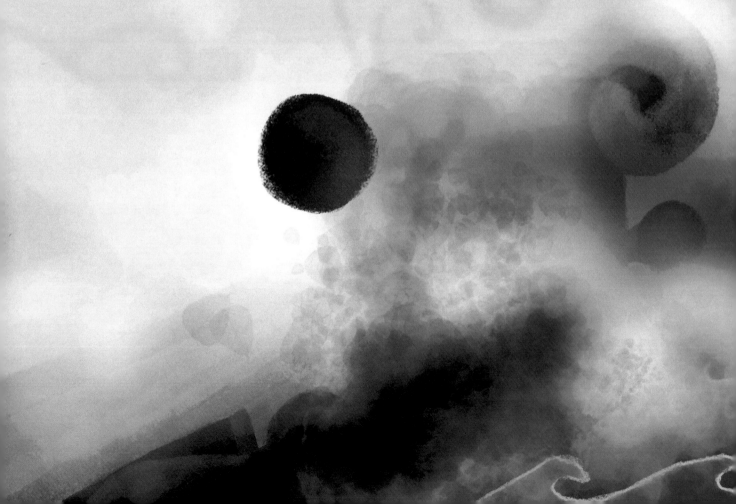

The battle was very fierce!

Jack wasn't entirely sure who won, but it was a lot of fun.

Machu laughed. "Because you've been in the bath tub and now the water is cold!"

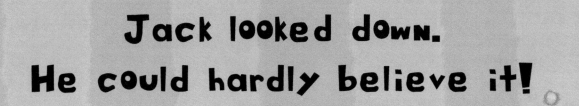

Jack looked down.
He could hardly believe it!

He had been so busy playing that he hadn't even noticed!

Later, when they were drying off with big, fluffy towels, Machu said to Jack. "I'm very proud of you! You were very brave."

Jack puffed up his chest and looked proud. "Of course I am. I am Jack the pirate kitten. I am very brave!"

And he was totally right.

THE END